JOE O'BRIEN is an award-winning gardener who lives in Ballyfermot in Dublin. This is his sixth book about the wonderful world of Alfie Green.

DEDICATION
The *Alfie Green* series is dedicated to my son, Ethan, who in his short time in this world taught me to be strong, happy and thankful for the gift of life. Thank you, Ethan, for the inspiration to write.

Alfie Green and the Conker King is dedicated to Aoife, Darragh and Jake.

ACKNOWLEDGEMENTS:
A big thank you to all at The O'Brien Press, to Jean Texier, and, of course, to my readers.

*   *   *

JEAN TEXIER is a storyboard artist and illustrator. Initially trained in animation, he has worked in the film industry for many years.

Alfie

and the CONKER KING

Green

Joe O'Brien

Illustrated by Jean Texier

THE O'BRIEN PRESS
DUBLIN

First published in hardback 2007 by The O'Brien Press Ltd.,
12 Terenure Road East, Rathgar, Dublin 6, Ireland.
Tel: +353 1 4923333; Fax: +353 1 4922777
E-mail: books@obrien.ie
Website: www.obrien.ie
This paperback edition first published 2011

ISBN: 978-1-84717-283-9

British Library Cataloguing-in-Publication Data
A catalogue record for this title is available from The British Library

2 3 4 5 6 7 8 9 10
11 12 13 14 15

The O'Brien Press receives
assistance from

Editing, typesetting, layout, design: The O'Brien Press Ltd.
Illustrations: Jean Texier
Printed and bound by CPI Cox and Wyman Ltd
The paper used in this book is produced using pulp from
managed forests

CONTENTS

CHAPTER 1

NEW RULES

Alfie and Fitzer were walking along the school corridor when they spotted Mr Moffet pinning something on the notice board.

Budsville Primary School
Team Conker Championship

RULES:

1. THREE PLAYERS TO A TEAM
2. BEST TWO OF EACH TEAM GOES FORWARD
3. NO BORROWING – PLAYERS MUST USE THEIR OWN CONKERS

'Hey!' said Alfie. 'They've changed it to a **team** contest.'

'Whacker Walsh won't be happy with that,' grinned Fitzer. Whacker had won the individual competition for the past two years.

Just then, Whacker and Emily Farrell nudged the two pals out of the way. 'A TEAM Competition? Huh! That won't stop me from winning! I'll have the best team in the school,' Whacker boasted.

He turned to Alfie. 'So, Green, who's going to be your third player?'

'Maybe it'll be Conor Hoolihan!' Emily suggested, and she and Whacker broke their sides laughing.

Alfie was
furious.

'That's
right, Emily.
Our third
player **IS** Conor
Hoolihan. See
you at the
games on Monday.'

Alfie walked off with his head held
high.

Fitzer ran after him. 'Alfie!' he
screeched. 'Have you gone **CONKERS
BONKERS**? Conor Hoolihan is the
worst conkers player in the whole of
Budsville.'

Fitzer was right. Conor Hoolihan
was so bad at conkers that his
nickname was 'Knuckles'. After every
conkers match his knuckles were
black and blue with bruises.
Sometimes he even
hit himself!

'Well,' Alfie said, 'I couldn't let Whacker have the last laugh. Anyway,' he added hopefully, 'maybe Conor will say no.'

But Conor didn't say no. He was **DELIGHTED** to be asked to join Alfie's team.

The three boys agreed to meet the next day in the park to pick their conkers for Monday.

CHAPTER 2

CONKER CHAOS!

When Alfie, Fitzer and Knuckles arrived in Laurel Park it was **TEEMING** with kids from school. There were only two horse chestnut trees and the conkers were disappearing fast. It was **Conker Chaos!**

'We'd better hurry, lads,' Knuckles said. 'All the good ones will be gone.'

Alfie noticed a cluster of really huge conkers at the very top of one of the trees.

'You two get some sticks, and I'll head over to that far tree to have a look,' he said.

Now, Alfie, as you know, can talk to plants and trees, so he leaned against the trunk of the tree and whispered, 'Excuse me, I don't suppose you could give me three of those really good conkers at the top, for the school championship?'

'**You kids**,' groaned the tree. 'Every year you turn up and throw sticks and rocks at us for our conkers, and then you leave without even a thank you.'

'Oh,' Alfie said, 'Sorry.'

He was just about to walk away when the chestnut tree shook itself.

Three HUGE conkers fell from the tree. As they hit the ground their shells exploded and out bounced three super-sized conkers.

'Thank you. Thank you very much,' Alfie called out.

'At least you *asked*,' said the tree.
'BUT DON'T COME BACK FOR MORE!'

Fitzer and Knuckles ran over.

'Wow!' Fitzer gasped.
'Deadly
conkers!
Where did
you find
them?'

'Oh, they
just fell out
of the sky!'
replied Alfie.
'Pure luck!'

The team went home to ask their dads to skewer the conkers and string them, so they could get C-R-A-C-K-I-N-G with polishing them for the championship on Monday.

CHAPTER 3

THAT'S CHEATING!

Alfie and Fitzer played their hearts out and won all of their matches.

Poor Knuckles lost every bout. He even picked up a few more bruises! But, as only two players from each team needed to win, Alfie's team found themselves in the grand final.

And who else was in the final? Whacker Walsh's team.

There was a break before the final and everyone headed for ice cream.

Willie Walsh was Whacker's dad. He had been a champion conker player and brought his ice-cream van to any match that Whacker played in.

As Alfie waited in the queue, he heard Whacker boasting to his dad how his team was going to **DEMOlish** Alfie's team in the final.

'It's no contest, Dad!' Whacker smirked.

'That's my boy!' Willie smiled.

Alfie noticed that the ice creams Willie gave Whacker, Emily and Adam Burke were bigger than anyone else's.

'Three ice creams with hundreds and thousands on top, Mr Walsh,' Alfie asked.

'Those are nasty bruises, Conor,' Willie Walsh remarked. 'Are you sure you'll be fit for the final?' He handed all three ice creams to Conor.

'**Careful**, Knuckles!' Alfie warned.

Conor struggled to hold on to everything.

Suddenly one of the ice creams slipped from his hand. He made a grab for it but it toppled to the ground, followed by his conker.

The conker landed near Whacker's shoe. He kicked it and it b**oun**ced off the tyre of the ice-cream van and rolled down a drain.

'Look what you did, Whacker!' shouted Alfie. 'That's **cheating**.'

'No. That's just bad luck,' laughed Willie Walsh.

Alfie, Fitzer and Knuckles were devastated. The rules were that a player without a conker must forfeit his game.

And you weren't allowed borrow from another player. So if Alfie or

Fitzer lost any of their final matches, Whacker's team would win.

But Alfie wasn't going to let them win by cheating.

'You wait here,' he told Fitzer and Knuckles. 'I'm going to get another conker for Conor.'

'But the park is cleaned out,' Fitzer reminded him. 'All the decent conkers are gone.'

'Trust me,' said Alfie, and he ran out the school gates and headed home.

CHAPTER 4

A PLAN

Alfie wasn't allowed home at break, so he snuck around the side of the house and crept into his shed.

He took the magical book from under the floorboards and placed his hand on the first page.

The wise old plant rose up from the book until it towered over Alfie.

Alfie tried to tell it everything without even stopping to breathe.

'We're in the final, and Whacker kicked Knuckles' conker down a shore, and ... '

'Slow down, Alfie,' begged the wise old plant. 'Now, what is it that you need?'

'A conker,' Alfie said. 'A really good conker.'

The wise old plant began to flick over the pages of the magical book,

until he came to a page that said 'Chestnut Woods'.

'Here we are,' he said, showing the page to Alfie.

'It's **disappearing**,' Alfie yelled.

Slowly but surely the words on the page changed from 'Chestnut Woods' to 'Skeleton Woods'.

CHESTNUT WOODS
SKELETON

The wise old plant was baffled.

'Well,' he said, 'I was going to suggest that you go to Chestnut Woods, where the best conkers in the world grow, but it seems to have vanished.'

'What am I going to do now?' Alfie asked. He was running out of time.

'You could try the Fungi Fields where the Marching Mushrooms live,' suggested the plant. 'The mushrooms used to march the Hairy Fairies all the way to Chestnut Woods for their great conker battles. If the mushrooms could find you a Hairy Fairy you just might get your conker.'

With that, the wise old plant folded itself back into the book, which closed with a

Alfie was stunned. **HAIRY FAIRIES** marching to conker battles on **MUSHROOMS??** He had seen a lot of strange things on his trips to Arcania, but this would surely be the strangest.

The only fairy Alfie had seen was
the one that his mother put on top of
the Christmas tree. And he couldn't
imagine her in a conker battle!

But there was no time to lose, so Alfie put the Crystal Orchid into his pocket, opened the shed door, and stepped out into Arcania.

CHAPTER 5

THE FUNGI FIELDS

'Hey! Alfie's back.'

Alfie heard the familiar voice of Paddy the spade.

'Anyone else around, Paddy?' Alfie asked.

'Just me,' answered Vinny the fork.

'Good to see you, lads,' Alfie said. 'Can you show me the way to the Fungi Fields? I'm in a bit of a hurry.'

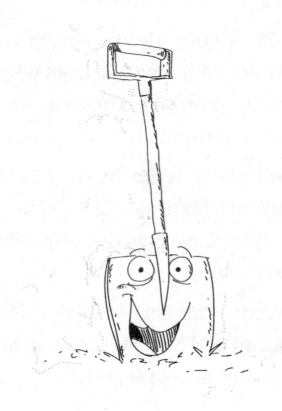

Paddy laughed. 'A **hurry**? Have you forgotten that time stands still while you are in Arcania?'

Alfie felt silly. He **had** forgotten. So he slowed down and told them all about the competition and why he needed a conker.

'It's a long way to the Fungi Fields,' Paddy said. 'And you have a match to play afterwards. Why don't you take a lift with Vinny?'

'Great,' Alfie hopped on to Vinny's back and held on tight as they pogoed all the way to the Fungi Fields.

The Fungi Fields were easy to
recognise because they were filled
with giant mushrooms. Most of them
seemed to be sleeping, with their giant
caps pulled down over their eyes.

'Excuse me,' Alfie stood on tiptoe
and tapped on the cap of a giant
mushroom.

45

'**Huh? What? Who?**' The mushroom woke with a start.

'I'm sorry to wake you,' Alfie apologised, but I'm looking for a Hairy Fairy.'

'A Hairy Fairy? Oh, dear, there used to be **lots** of them around here,' said the mushroom, 'but I'm afraid they're all gone now. Every single one of them. No need for them to be here. They don't need us any more to march them to Chestnut Woods, or should I say, Skeleton Woods.'

CHAPTER 6

Skeleton Woods

'Why? What happened to the woods?' Alfie asked.

'The Chestnut Woods caught fire from a lightning bolt during the Great Storm, and every tree perished,' the mushroom explained. 'All  that was left were tree skeletons. There were no more conkers and the great

conker battles of the Hairy Fairies ceased.'

Alfie was gutted, but he wasn't going to give up.

'Can you take me to Skeleton Woods?' he asked the mushroom.

'Well,' said the mushroom, 'I suppose I could. I have nothing better to do. And I could do with the exercise.'

The giant mushroom leaned over and Alfie jumped aboard.

He waved goodbye to Vinny. 'Thanks for the lift, Vinny.'

'Any time, Alfie,' Vinny answered as they disappeared into the distance.

Travelling on the Marching Mushroom wasn't as much fun as springing along with Vinny, but the mushroom kept Alfie entertained with stories of the great conker battles of the past. They used to last for weeks, and the final winner would be crowned Conker King.

Soon Alfie could see row after row of tree skeletons. Their bare branches pointed up at the sky, like the bony fingers of a skeleton. He shivered.

One tree was different.
It seemed to be covered
entirely in
snow-white
leaves, which
blew in the
wind,
only there was
no wind.
It was a
G-H-O-S-T
TREE.

Suddenly
its arms lifted.

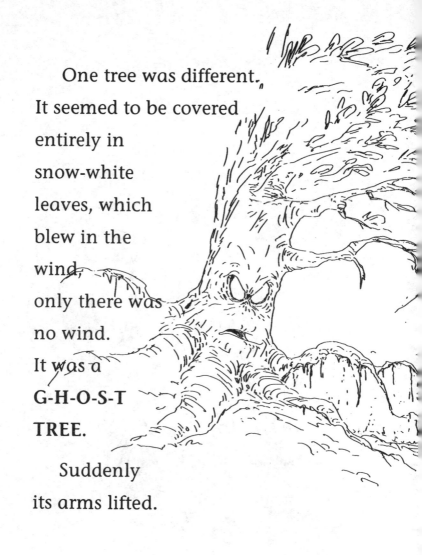

'Who is this approaching Skeleton Woods?' the ghost tree asked, in a high, rustly voice.

The Marching Mushroom leaned over and Alfie slid down to the ground.

'I'm Alfie Green and this is ...'

But the mushroom had already marched off. Alfie was **alone** with the ghost tree. He stood very straight and tried to stop his knees from knocking.

'You're a very brave young man,' said the tree. 'No one comes to Skeleton Woods any more. What brings you here?'

'I ... I'm here to find a Hairy Fairy to ask it for a conker.'

'Well,' said the tree, 'you might be in luck. There is one – and only one – of the great conker battlers left in the woods.'

'Really?' Alfie was delighted.

The ghost tree pointed. 'Somewhere in there is the Conker King. The greatest of all conker battlers will not leave his battlegrounds. Not now, not ever.'

Then the leaves of the ghost tree disappeared into its branches, leaving only a skeleton.

CHAPTER 7

TICKLY MOSS

Following the ghost tree's directions, Alfie headed deep into the woods in search of the Conker King.

For a long time he walked on crunchy, twitchy ground of dead twigs. Then the path beneath his feet became softer, fluffier and very quiet.

'Lovely,' Alfie sighed as the thick moss cushioned his feet like a really expensive hotel carpet.

It almost felt like his feet were sinking into the cushion.

His feet **WERE** sinking! Then his legs disappeared. And then he was in it up to his knees.

'Hey! What's happening?' Alfie yelled. **'Ha, ha. Hee, hee, hee ... '**

The moss began to tickle. And tickle. And tickle.

Although Alfie knew he was in real

danger, he couldn't stop laughing.

'Ho, ho. Tee, hee, hee … '

Soon his waist was beneath the tickly carpet. Alfie tried to reach into his pocket for his Crystal Orchid, but the moss tickled him so much that he had to take his hands back out.

Alfie waved his arms in desperation. 'Help!' he shouted. 'Help!'

Alfie felt something wrapping around him. Then he was being pulled out of the thick, quick, tickly moss. His feet left the ground and he found himself up a tree, looking at the strangest creature he had ever seen.

It was half the size of Alfie but its hands and feet were enormous and covered in hair. It had a long crooked nose and big bulging eyes.

On its extra-hairy head it wore a crown made from twisted twigs and spiny chestnut shells. It must be the Conker King!

The Conker King had lassoed his conker around Alfie, and pulled off the perfect tangler.

Alfie was still gasping for breath.

'That ... was ... weird,' he said to his rescuer. 'I've never been in so much danger and laughed so much at the same time.'

The Conker King untied his powerful conker from around Alfie. Instantly the string shortened back to normal length.

'Wow!' said Alfie. 'You really are the true king of conkers.'

The Conker King was pleased. It had been a long time since anyone had called him that.

CHAPTER 8

THE CONKER KING

Alfie told the Conker King all about his quest and how he desperately needed a conker for the competition back home.

Without hesitation, the Conker King handed Alfie the conker and string that had rescued him.

'Take this. I'll never use it in battle again,' said the Conker King.

Alfie had his conker. 'Thank you so much,' he said.

'Now, how will you get home?' asked the Conker King.

'Ah,' Alfie said, 'I have a secret!' He took out the Crystal Orchid and grasped it tightly.

There was a flash of blinding light.

He was home again.

He was just in time. The finals were about to begin.

'Where have you been, Alfie?'
Fitzer asked anxiously. 'Whacker was
telling everyone that you were afraid
to turn up.'

'Oh, was he?' Alfie laughed. 'We'll show him who's afraid!'

He gave the Conker King's conker to Knuckles. 'Here you are, Conor.'

'What a beauty!' Knuckles gasped. 'Where did you get it?'

'Eh, let's just say it comes from a very distant hero of mine.'

Fitzer beat Emily Farrell and now it was Alfie's turn against Whacker. Adam Burke was drawn last against Knuckles.

But before Alfie could raise his conker, Principal Boggins had something to say.

'Alfie Green is disqualified for leaving the school grounds without permission.'

Whacker had squealed on Alfie!

Principal Boggins went on, 'Jason Walsh is disqualified for kicking Conor's conker down the drain.'

Fitzer had squealed on Whacker!

It was all square.

CHAPTER 9

COME ON, KNUCKLES!

Alfie wrapped the string around Knuckles' hand and slapped him on the back.

'Come on, Conor. Believe in your conker and believe in yourself, and you'll beat him.'

'Go on, Knuckles,' shouted Fitzer. 'You can do it.'

Conor was shaking. 'We're going to lose, lads,' he said.

Adam Burke won the toss to strike first.

'Prepare for pain,' he said as he swung his conker down at Knuckles' shaking hand.

The two conkers clashed, but there wasn't even a mark on Knuckles' conker.

And there wasn't a mark on his knuckles either.

But Whacker was still grinning. He **knew** that Adam would get him the next time.

Now it was Knuckles' turn.

He swung his conker back and, as he did, the string s-t-r-e-t-c-h-e-d until the conker stopped in mid air. Poor Conor was balancing on one leg.

Then, like a bolt of lightning –

SMASH!

Adam's conker burst into **SMITHEREENS.**

The explosion flung him, backwards, knocking Whacker Walsh and Emily Farrell to the ground.

Principal Boggins lifted Knuckles' arm into the air.

'I declare Conor Hoolihan **THE WINNER!**'

They had done it! Alfie, Fitzer and Knuckles were the Conker Champions of Budsville School.

They held their trophy high as all the kids cheered them on.

'To the Conker King!' shouted Alfie.

'Is that your distant hero, Alfie?' asked Knuckles.

'No, Conor, it's you,' replied a smiling Alfie.

READ ALFIE'S OTHER GREAT ADVENTURES IN:

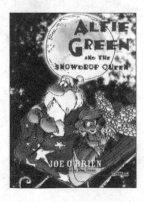

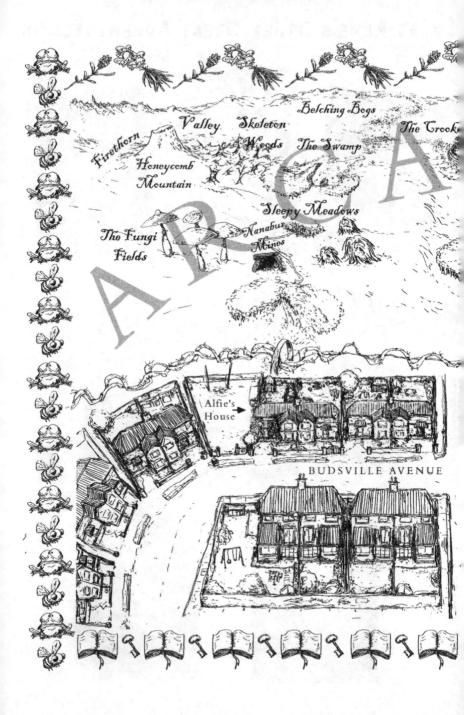

Belching Bogs

Valley   Skeleton

Firethorn   Woods   The Swamp   The Crook

Honeycomb
Mountain

Sleepy Meadows

The Fungi   Nanabur
Fields   Mines

Alfie's
House

BUDSVILLE AVENUE

The
Wonderful World of
Alfie Green

SYCAMORE ROAD

LAUREL PARK

BUDSVILLE
PRIMARY
SCHOOL

On his ninth birthday
Alfie Green got a very special
present – a magical book left
by his grandad.

The book gives Alfie special
powers and opens a whole new
wonderful world ...

MA

Please return/renew this item by the last date shown